PUFFIN BOOKS

PUGWASH AND THE MIDNIGHT FEAST
and
PUGWASH AND THE WRECKERS

'Plundering porpoises! I suppose I ought to put you all in irons!' cried Captain Pugwash, on discovering his crew about to tuck into a tasty midnight feast. Luckily for the crew, Pugwash decides to join in the feast instead! But then *more* uninvited guests drop in – and a most unwelcome bunch they are too . . . Cut-throat Jake and his bloodthirsty band of buccaneers! They tie up the crew of the *Black Pig* and gobble up their feast in front of their very eyes! However, there's a surprise in store for Jake and his evil gang – the mysterious islanders from nearby Rummi-Tummi are on their way!

And in the second of these two exciting stories, Captain Pugwash is in jovial mood. He's about to set sail for the Indies with the greatest load of silver bullion ever! But Pugwash's evil arch-enemy, Cut-throat Jake, overhears his plans and is determined to wreck the *Black Pig* . . .

John Ryan's jolly captain is as bumbling and amusing as ever in these two pirate stories.

D0714471

PUGWASH
and the
MIDNIGHT
FEAST

and

PUGWASH
and the
WRECKERS

JOHN RYAN

Puffin Books

Puffin Books, Penguin Books Ltd, Harmondsworth, Middlesex, England
Viking Penguin Inc., 40 West 23rd Street, New York, New York 10010, U.S.A.
Penguin Books Australia Ltd, Ringwood, Victoria, Australia
Penguin Books Canada Limited, 2801 John Street, Markham, Ontario, Canada L4R 1B4
Penguin Books (N.Z.) Ltd, 182–190 Wairau Road, Auckland 10, New Zealand

Captain Pugwash and the Midnight Feast
first published by The Bodley Head Ltd, 1984
Captain Pugwash and the Wreckers
first published by The Bodley Head, 1984
Published in one volume in Puffin Books 1986

Copyright © John Ryan, 1984, 1986
All rights reserved

Made and printed in Great Britain by
Richard Clay (The Chaucer Press) Ltd, Bungay, Suffolk
Typeset in Ehrhardt

Except in the United States of America,
this book is sold subject to the condition
that it shall not, by way of trade or otherwise,
be lent, re-sold, hired out, or otherwise circulated
without the publisher's prior consent in any form of
binding or cover other than that in which it is
published and without a similar condition
including this condition being imposed
on the subsequent purchaser

PUGWASH
and the
MIDNIGHT
FEAST

and

PUGWASH
and the
WRECKERS

JOHN RYAN

Puffin Books

Puffin Books, Penguin Books Ltd, Harmondsworth, Middlesex, England
Viking Penguin Inc., 40 West 23rd Street, New York, New York 10010, U.S.A.
Penguin Books Australia Ltd, Ringwood, Victoria, Australia
Penguin Books Canada Limited, 2801 John Street, Markham, Ontario, Canada L4R 1B4
Penguin Books (N.Z.) Ltd, 182–190 Wairau Road, Auckland 10, New Zealand

Captain Pugwash and the Midnight Feast
first published by The Bodley Head Ltd, 1984
Captain Pugwash and the Wreckers
first published by The Bodley Head, 1984
Published in one volume in Puffin Books 1986

Copyright © John Ryan, 1984, 1986
All rights reserved

Made and printed in Great Britain by
Richard Clay (The Chaucer Press) Ltd, Bungay, Suffolk
Typeset in Ehrhardt

Except in the United States of America,
this book is sold subject to the condition
that it shall not, by way of trade or otherwise,
be lent, re-sold, hired out, or otherwise circulated
without the publisher's prior consent in any form of
binding or cover other than that in which it is
published and without a similar condition
including this condition being imposed
on the subsequent purchaser

PUGWASH
and the
MIDNIGHT
FEAST

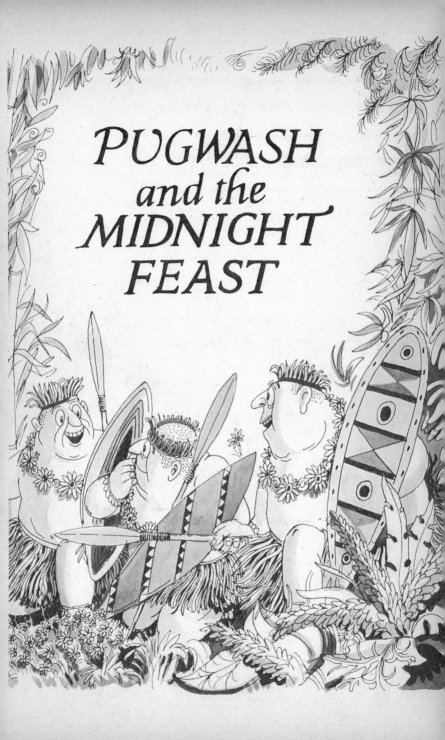

It was a warm, sleepy afternoon on the
Pacific island of Rummi-Tummi
and at the end of a long
and tiring journey,
the *Black Pig* lay at
anchor in the bay.

High on the poop-deck, Captain Pugwash was
peacefully asleep in his hammock . . . or rather,
he was *pretending* to be peacefully asleep . . .

. . . pretending, because at the other end of the ship, he had noticed that his crew were behaving in an exceedingly suspicious manner. For one thing, they were awake instead of having their afternoon snooze—

and the fact that Tom the cabin boy was with them made the Captain even more worried.

"Now, mess-mates," said the Mate. "We must make sure all our preparations are in order . . ."

9

And in spite of their warnings, Tom climbed
down into the dinghy.

Soon he was rowing to the shore of
Rummi-Tummi Island . . .

. . . and two hours later, safe and sound, and
with a heavy boatload, he was on his way back.

But Barnabas was right—
the Captain *was* suspicious.

Indeed, when he climbed
into bed that night, he
kept all his clothes on!

At first, all was quiet
on board the *Black Pig*.

Then as eight bells struck for midnight . . .

. . . the pirates jumped straight out of their bunks and gathered round the mess-table to enjoy their carefully prepared . . .

. . . MIDNIGHT FEAST!

"My goodness, you've done us proud this time!" said the Mate, as they surveyed the table. It was spread with all sorts of tasty foods and

delicious island fruits and vegetables.

"Aye, and there's plenty of it too!" said Willy happily.

"Lucky we didn't ask the Captain," said Barnabas. "He'd have eaten the lot—and all by 'isself too!"

"Indeed, Pirate Barnabas . . ." said a voice from the door.

And there, as the pirates turned in confusion and surprise . . .

OH NO!

OH MY!

OH DEAR!

. . . stood their Captain, looking particularly pleased with himself.

"Plundering porpoises!" he cried.

"I suppose I ought to put you all in irons! Or maybe make you write out one hundred times:—

"'We must *not* have midnight feasts on board ship!' But no . . . I feel unusually kindly today!

"So, instead of punishing you, I shall JOIN you!"
"But . . . but . . . but . . ." cried the Mate anxiously.

RUM PLEASE, TOM!

But Pugwash was already happily tucking in and for the pirates there was nothing to do but make the best of it. After all, he *was* their Captain.

Soon everybody was
busy eating and pouring
out drinks and proposing
toasts.

GOOD
HEALTH!

And nobody
noticed that some *more* uninvited guests
were coming to the midnight feast . . .

. . . guests whose ship had
dropped anchor close by
that evening, under
cover of darkness . . .

. . . and who were now scrambling up
the side of the *Black Pig*. They were
the most unwelcome guests of all—

—Cut-throat Jake
and his desperate band
of bloodthirsty buccaneers!

Captain Pugwash had just helped himself to
a second scrumptious sandwich
when suddenly—

—Cut-throat Jake and his gang rushed in and surrounded the pirates.

HAH!

"'Avin' a midnight feast, eh?" roared Jake, "and never thought of askin' *us* to join you? Well, we're 'ere now, you greedy old ruffian, and we wouldn't *dream* of not askin' you to join *us*!

"Tied up, you'll be, where you can watch *us* finishing off your fancy goodies! And after that it'll be the plank for the lot of 'ee . . . so the sharks can have *their* midnight feast too!"

And very soon Jake had Captain Pugwash and the Mate and Barnabas and Willy and Tom all tied together back to back—

—and dumped on the mess-table, so that they
could all see their captors hungrily gobbling up

all the food in sight.

And so, for the *third*
time that night . . .

. . . a merry party was under way on board the *Black Pig* . . .

. . . so merry that
again nobody noticed . . .

that yet *more* uninvited guests were
on their way.

Two great canoes had
approached silently from the
island and the islanders who
came in them were now
silently scrambling up the
sides of the *Black Pig*.

Suddenly the foc's'le was filled with leaping, yelling figures who seized Jake and his crew.

They untied Pugwash and the Mate and Barnabas and Willy and Tom and carried them all out, struggling and kicking . . .

up on to the deck, down over the side of
the ship, and into the two great canoes

in which they were then swiftly propelled
towards the beach.

The whole attack had happened so suddenly
that at first the pirates were stunned. Only
Tom didn't seem to be particularly surprised
at the turn of events. Then Barnabas spoke:

"If you ask me, mess-mates," he said, "the
real midnight feast is taking place on shore
tonight. And you know wot could be on
the menu? . . . Pirate pie and chips!"

"Coddling catfish! They can't!" cried the
Captain.

"Can't they just," muttered the Mate.

Tom didn't say anything, but it looked as though Barnabas was right. Up on the beach hundreds of islanders were gathering round a big fire with a large cooking pot on it.

"Let's hope they'll cook Jake first," whispered Pugwash.

Soon the whole party was set ashore on the beach. "Maybe he'll give them such indigestion they won't fancy any more!" said the Captain.

But Jake and his men were led away to a large hut some distance off . . .

. . . whereas Pugwash and his crew were taken up to a high throne on which what looked like the King of the island was sitting.

When they got there, wreaths of flowers were placed round their necks.

"Garnish! that's what that is!" grunted Barnabas.

And Captain Pugwash became so terrified that
he cried, "Let us go at once, I say! I demand
to see the British Consul! I . . . I . . ."
But the King interrupted him
with a broad smile.

"My dear Captain,"
he said, "what on
earth is troubling
you? There's no
need to look so
anxious.

"It's like this.

When I met your cabin
boy Tom on the island
this afternoon, he told me that a midnight
feast was planned for this evening and
I thought what fun it would be to prepare
a really splendid banquet for you here
on the island, as a surprise.

"And that is what we've done. I'm so sorry that we had to board your ship and bring you back here in such a rude manner. But the arrival of that ruffian Jake—who your cabin boy tells me is one of the vilest villains afloat— left me no choice. Never fear, I shall keep them under very close guard tonight and hand them over to the proper authorities in the morning."

And so, as Jake and his crew crouched
miserably in their prison hut, cursing and
swearing and not having the slightest idea
of what was going to happen to them . . .

Captain Pugwash and the Mate and Barnabas and
Willy and Tom the cabin boy settled down . . .

. . . to the most delicious dinner they had ever
eaten in their lives.

"Goodness me!" remarked the King. "What a fearful noise your enemies are making!"

For by now the yelling and cursing from Jake and his crew could be heard all over the island.

"I shouldn't worry too much about them," said Captain Pugwash happily.

"They have probably got some *extraordinary*
idea that they're being kept in store specially . . .

. . . for breakfast!"

PUGWASH
and the
WRECKERS

"Fill up everybody's glasses, Landlord!" cried Captain Pugwash. "The drinks are on *me* today!"

There was an astonished silence. The scene was the Buccaneers' Arms where it was well known that the Captain was far too mean to stand a drink to anybody!

But today was different.

"You see," went on the Captain, "I am for once working for His Majesty's Government! Tonight the good ship *Black Pig* sets forth to the Indies with the greatest load of silver bullion ever to leave these shores. And why? . . . because the Navy ship contracted to do the job has been delayed and the silver is needed urgently to pay our gallant soldiers. We sail tonight on the eight o'clock tide, me hearties. Let us drink to a successful voyage!"

Unseen in the snug-bar next door, Cut-throat Jake, the Captain's worst enemy, held out his tankard for a filling of free rum, and chuckled . . .

"Successful voyage indeed," he growled to his mates. "Ho, ho, ho! He'll get no further than the Barnacle Reef if *I* have anything to do with it! Gather round, lads, and listen to me plan. We have no time to lose! No time even to return to the *Flying Dustman* . . ."

Now the Barnacle Reef lay at the mouth of the harbour. Many a ship had been wrecked on its dreaded, razor-sharp rocks . . . so many that a great light-house had been built on the Reef to warn vessels at night to steer clear.

And it so happened that the keeper of the light-house was none other than Tom the cabin boy's Uncle Joe. In fact, as Pugwash and his crew returned to their ship, and Jake and his men sneaked away to their longboat . . .

. . . Tom had gone to take
tea with his Uncle Joe
in the living-room of the
light-house. They were old
friends and it was a
chance for Tom to say
goodbye to his uncle

GOOD TO
SEE YOU, TOM,
ME BOY!

before setting out
with Captain Pugwash
on the journey to
the Indies.

"And now, Tom," said
Uncle Joe, "before you
go, I'll take you upstairs
and show you the
light-house lamp."

So Tom followed
his uncle . . .

. . . and when they got upstairs, he was shown
the huge oil light which had saved so many
ships from wrecking on the Barnacle Reef.

"Usually," said his uncle, "I light the lamp by hand when dusk comes down. But if for any reason I have to be away until later, I have worked out a timing device. I have this candle which will last for one, two or three hours. When the candle burns down it sets fire to this short length of fuse which in turn lights the wick of the lamp, at any time I want it."

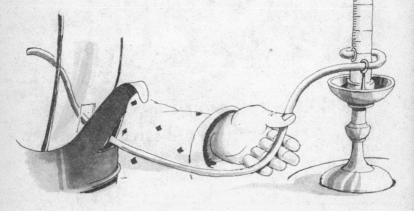

Suddenly Joe broke off. "That's funny," he said. "I thought I heard voices downstairs. It sounds as though we have visitors. Wait now, while I go down and see."

LISTEN!

And Joe climbed down the ladder from the lamp room to the living-room . . .

. . . straight into the clutches of Cut-throat Jake and his desperate band who had just arrived in their longboat. In a moment they had him tied up and lashed to his own chair.

"Now, Mr Light-house Keeper," growled Jake, "stay quiet, and you'll come to no harm. But there's some that will, ho, ho, ho! for when dusk comes down tonight, there'll be

no guiding light on the Barnacle Reef
— 'cos *you'll* not be able to move to light it.
There'll be a false light lit by a friend o' mine
further out to sea.
And that means
that any ship . . .

(and there's
one *very special*
ship . . . ha, ha,
harhh!) that sails from
the port tonight will smash
on the rocks as sure as eggs is eggs!

"Now that ship belongs to that old
ruffian Pugwash,
and it has a very
special cargo aboard—
a cargo o' silver bullion.
And guess who'll
be waiting on the
rocks to grab it and
put paid to the ship's
worthless crew . . . why . . . yours untruly,
o' course. Come on, me handsomes.
Let's finish off the tea.
We'll need our bellies
full for the dirty
work ahead!"

And the ruffians were so busy
gobbling down what remained
of the crumpets and cakes

that they never noticed Tom's signal
to his uncle from the hatch above . . . nor
Tom's escape down a rope *outside* the
light-house . . . and they heard nothing as he
rowed himself quietly back towards the harbour.

Meanwhile, on board the
Black Pig, Captain Pugwash
was trying to get his ship
under way to catch the
evening tide. "Cast her off!"
he cried. "Hoist the sails . . .
Make for the open sea!"

"But I can't remember
how to untie the knots,"
complained Willy.

"I'm in a bit of
a tangle meself,"
grunted Barnabas.

"Fact is, we'll not get nowhere without Tom!" said the Mate. Which was true. Tom really was the only one who knew how to work the ship.

"Weeping walruses!" cried the Captain angrily. "Where *is* the wretched boy?!"

But Tom hadn't gone straight back to the
Black Pig from the light-house. For one
thing he wanted to see where Jake had moored
his ship in the harbour.

The sun was setting behind the
Barnacle Reef when at last he brought the
dinghy back to his own vessel.

AHOY THERE,
BLACK
PIG !!

"Tom! Thank heavens you're—I mean where on earth have you been?" The Captain corrected himself angrily. "We can't wait all night, you know!"

"Sorry, Cap'n," said Tom.

"Something's turned up and we're going to have to alter our plans a bit!" And because he knew he couldn't sail without Tom, the Captain had to listen.

An hour later, darkness had fallen. But no warning light shone from the light-house on the treacherous Barnacle Reef. Instead a false light beamed from a point further out to sea.

Among the jagged
rocks, Cut-throat Jake and
his bloodthirsty crew
watched . . . and waited . . .
and scanned the murky,
moonlit sea with greedy
eyes.

Time passed . . . tension mounted . . .

Then, from the direction of the harbour a
faint shape could be seen approaching through
the gloom. At first it
was no more than a
shadow . . . then
at last . . .

IT'S A
SHIP!

IT *MUST* BE
THE *BLACK
PIG* !!

Sure enough,
a large vessel was
coming into sight.

As Jake and his
crew crouched
excitedly among the
rocks they could hear
the creaking of the
rigging and the swirl
of the waves round
the bows.

"At any moment
now she'll strike the
Reef," breathed
Jake. "Stand by with
your cutlasses,
me beauties . . ."

Then suddenly, with
a flicker and a flash . . .

the lamp of the Barnacle
light-house burst alight
above them, and in the
sudden blaze the
horrified ruffians saw . . .

. . . the bows of the approaching vessel rise and fall on the waves, then strike on the rocks with a fearful rending crash.

But the name they saw on the prow was NOT *Black Pig*—

THAT'S NOT **PUGWASH'S** SHIP!

IT'S **OURS!!**

for it was Cut-throat Jake's own ship
that had struck the Barnacle Reef!
And for Jake, even worse was to follow.

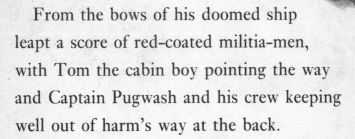

From the bows of his doomed ship
leapt a score of red-coated militia-men,
with Tom the cabin boy pointing the way
and Captain Pugwash and his crew keeping
well out of harm's way at the back.

Dazzled by the sudden glare, bewildered
by the unexpected turn of events, Jake and
his crew put up little resistance. Very soon
they were rounded up, and marched away . . .

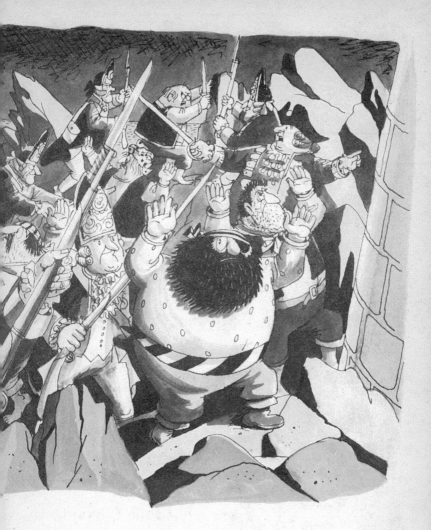

. . . into the light-house, where . . .

Tom's Uncle Joe was released and Jake and his men were put in irons.

"Dashed grateful to you, sir!" said the Officer in Charge to Captain Pugwash, "for leading us to these desperate criminals!"

"Think nothing of it. Glad to be of service . . . especially if there's a reward attached!" replied the Captain, slightly out of breath.

And he boasted all the way, of course . . .

as Tom and his uncle rowed him and the crew
back to the harbour, leaving the militia in
charge of the light-house and the prisoners,
and the *Flying Dustman* firmly stuck
on the rocks.

"Smart work, Tom," whispered Uncle Joe. "I know it was you who fixed it all — but it beats me how you did it."

"Easy, Uncle," said Tom. "When Jake and his crew grabbed you, I first set the lamp to light at about eight this evening in the way you showed me. Then I escaped down the *outside* of the light-house."

"But why didn't your Captain sail out on the evening tide?" interrupted Joe. "How was it that it was *Jake's* ship that went on the rocks?"

"Well," said Tom, in a lowered voice, "the crew of the *Black Pig* really aren't much good at getting the ship going *without* me. So all I had to do was to find out where Jake's ship was moored, tell the Captain to alert the soldiers, and then we all got on board the *Flying Dustman*, cast her loose on the falling tide, and sailed her on to the Barnacle Reef."

"This calls for a celebration," cried Captain Pugwash as they landed from the long-boat and made for the Buccaneers' Arms.

And so, for the second time that day . . .

there were free drinks
all round at the
Captain's expense.

He even ordered a lemonade
for Tom the cabin boy . . .

and told everybody how brave he, Captain Pugwash, had been in leading the militia in their attack on the wreckers of Barnacle Reef.

So a merry evening was had by all, and it was not until the following day . . .

that the *Black Pig* at last set out on the
Captain's voyage to the Indies. Cut-throat
Jake and his men were safely in the town
gaol, awaiting trial for attempted wrecking,
and as there was indeed a reward for Jake's
capture, Pugwash was even better off than
he had been before.

"'Bye-bye, Tom!" shouted Uncle Joe from the top of the Barnacle light-house. "Have a good journey! You *ought* to be all right with a skilful Captain like yours!"

"Smart fellow, your uncle!" said Captain Pugwash as he steered the ship well clear of the Reef.

"Knows a good man when he sees one . . . eh?"

But even at that distance Tom could see that his uncle was winking, and he waved and smiled . . . and said nothing.

Some other Young Puffins

PUGWASH AND THE MUTINY and PUGWASH AND THE FANCY-DRESS PARTY
John Ryan

Another pair of amazing adventures of the much-loved Captain Pugwash in which he is rescued from tricky situations by cabin-boy Tom.

THE CONKER AS HARD AS A DIAMOND
Chris Powling

A lively title for a really lively book! Little Alpesh's burning ambition is to find a diamond-hard conker, to make him champion of the universe. A zany story, sparkling with fun, to delight conker fiends.

ELOISE
Kay Thompson

At the Plaza Hotel, surrounded by her dog, her turtle, her nanny and a host of hotel guests, six-year-old Eloise is never bored . . .

ANNA, GRANDPA AND THE BIG STORM
Carla Stevens

Anna is just as determined as her usually grumpy Grandpa that she should get to school. It's the final of the spelling competition and she wants to be there. But as they struggle through the snow while the blizzard grows stronger and stronger, Anna begins to wonder whether they will ever get there. And when their train becomes snowbound, she begins to wonder whether they will ever get home again!

THE SNOW KITTEN
Nina Warner Hooke

Bewildered and hungry, the kitten wandered round the village hopelessly seeking food and shelter until it seemed as if his sad little life would end without ever having properly begun. But the children cared, and tried to work a miracle in time for Christmas.

TALES FROM THE WIND IN THE WILLOWS
Kenneth Grahame

Mole thought life along the riverbank might be a little dull, but he couldn't have been more wrong. There were all sorts of animals living in and by the river, and one in particular who was anything *but* dull – Mr Toad. A new edition of this classic story about Mole, Water Rat, Badger and Toad, illustrated by Margaret Gordon and especially abridged for younger readers.

CUP FINAL FOR CHARLIE
Joy Allen

Two stories about a cheerful young boy, Charlie. In the first, Charlie is thrilled with his birthday present from Uncle Tim – a cup final ticket! And in the second, Boots for Charlie, he goes on a fishing trip wearing another birthday present – a new pair of wellies.

THE RAILWAY CAT
Phyllis Arkle

Alfie the Railway Cat lives at the railway station. The cattiness begins with Hack, the porter who can't abide Alfie, devising a plan to get rid of the cat for good, at the same time obliging an actor friend of his who is looking for a pantomime cat!

DINNER LADIES DON'T COUNT
Bernard Ashley

Two stories set in a school. Jason has to prove he didn't take Donna's birthday cards and Linda tells a lie about why she can't go on the school outing.

TALES FROM ALLOTMENT LANE SCHOOL
Margaret Joy

A collection of twelve lively stories set in the reception class of a primary school. Miss Mee and her mixed class of five-year-olds have a series of day-to-day experiences, which make extremely entertaining and humorous reading.

THREE CHEERS FOR RAGDOLLY ANNA
Jean Kenward

Made only from a morsel of this and a tatter of that, Ragdolly Anna is a very special doll. Her adventures were serialized for television.

HAIRY AND SLUG
Margaret Joy

Meet Slug – a battered old car with a personality – and Hairy, an extremely shaggy mongrel addicted to television. They both belong to an ordinary family, with two children, and together they make up a hilarious combination of fun and adventure.

RETURN TO OZ
L. Frank Baum and Alistair Hedley

Dorothy knows that her friends and the Emerald City must be saved from the evil Nome King, the cruel Princess Mombi and the terrifying squealing Wheelers. So, with some strange companions, Tik-Tok, Jack Pumpkinhead and a talking hen, Billina, she sets off on a frightening, mysterious and exciting adventure.

THE TALE OF GREYFRIARS BOBBY
Lavinia Derwent

A specially retold version for younger readers, of the true story of a little Skye terrier who was faithful to his master even in death.

LITTLE DOG LOST
Nina Warner Hooke

The adventures of Pepito, a scruffy black and white puppy who lives in an old soap powder box in Spain. The excitement starts when the rubbish collectors sweep Pepito up in his box and deposit him at the bottom of a disused quarry, miles from anywhere!